Pablo's Feelings

Pablo created by Gráinne Mc Guinness
Written by Sumita Majumdar and Andrew Brenner

LADYBIRD BOOKS

UK | USA | Canada | Ireland | Australia | India | New Zealand | South Africa

Ladybird Books is part of the Penguin Random House group of companies
whose addresses can be found at global.penguinrandomhouse.com.

www.penguin.co.uk   www.puffin.co.uk   www.ladybird.co.uk

 Penguin
Random House
UK

First published 2020
001

PAPER ⊙WL FILMS

Printed in China

A CIP catalogue record for this book is available from the British Library

ISBN: 978-0-241-41576-4

All correspondence to:
Ladybird Books
Penguin Random House Children's
One Embassy Gardens, New Union Square
5 Nine Elms Lane, London SW8 5DA

MIX
Paper from
responsible sources
FSC® C018179
FSC
www.fsc.org

Tang

Noa

Draff

I'm Pablo!

Llama

Mouse   Wren

These are my friends, the Book Animals!
The Book Animals live in the Art World,
where I draw my stories.

One day, I was using my yellow crayon to draw a picture of Wren, when I heard Mum say some words. "Would you like to go and see your cousin Lorna today, Pablo?"

"Hooray!" I thought. "I like cousin Lorna!"
But then I heard Mum say some more words
into her phone . . .

"Sorry, Lorna. He doesn't
look like he wants to go
today. Maybe another time,"
she said. "Not today."

Not today?
What does
that mean?

I didn't understand why
Mum had said that,
but I carried on drawing
Wren in a tree. She was
singing my favourite song!
Then I drew Mouse.

"What's wrong, Pablo?" asked Mouse.
"Why is your face doing that?"
"Doing **what?**" I asked.
"Your mouth looks sad," said Mouse.

Then Noasaurus and Llama arrived.
"Are you **angry?**" asked Noa.
"Are you **angry?**" repeated Llama.

I didn't know why everyone thought
I was angry. I wasn't angry. Wren
was singing my favourite Wren song.

Mouse drew a picture to show me what my face was doing. I looked at it. "What's wrong with **him?**" I asked.

"That's a drawing of your face, Pablo," said Noa.
"But my face isn't doing that . . . is it?" I asked.
"Yes," said Mouse. "That's why Mouse drew it."

Then Mouse showed me a **mirror**.

"In point of fact, the Mirror Face is a reflection of your face," explained Draff. "It shows exactly what you look like."

I looked at the angry face in the mirror.

I didn't think it looked like me at all!

"The Mirror Face looks cross! And I'm happy!" I said.
"The Mirror Face isn't showing what I **feel** like."
"That means **your face** isn't showing what you feel
like either," said Mouse.

"Maybe that's why Mum thought I didn't
want to play with Lorna today," I said.
"Because of what my face was doing."

"Sorry!" said the Mirror Face. "I didn't know
what to do. I was just doing what you were doing."

"What's going on?" asked Tang, as he hurried over to join us.
"I think Pablo's face is **broken**," said Noa.
"He's feeling happy, but his face isn't showing it."

"When I'm happy, my face does things like **this!**" said Tang, pulling the corners of his mouth into a smile.

Tang made lots of **silly** faces and I laughed.

"Your face looks happy now!" said Mouse.

But as soon as I stopped laughing at Tang's silly faces, Mouse said I looked angry again.
I wasn't angry. I was happy!
"How can we help Pablo's face?" asked Noa.

I decided to put a big book in front of my face, so my face couldn't tell people things that I wasn't feeling.

"Mouse can't see Pablo's face if you do that," said Mouse.
"And we like your face," said Wren. "Give it another chance!"

"Your face can do **lots of things!**" said Tang, trying to be helpful. "Your face can look cross, surprised, sad, happy, frightened, confused . . ."

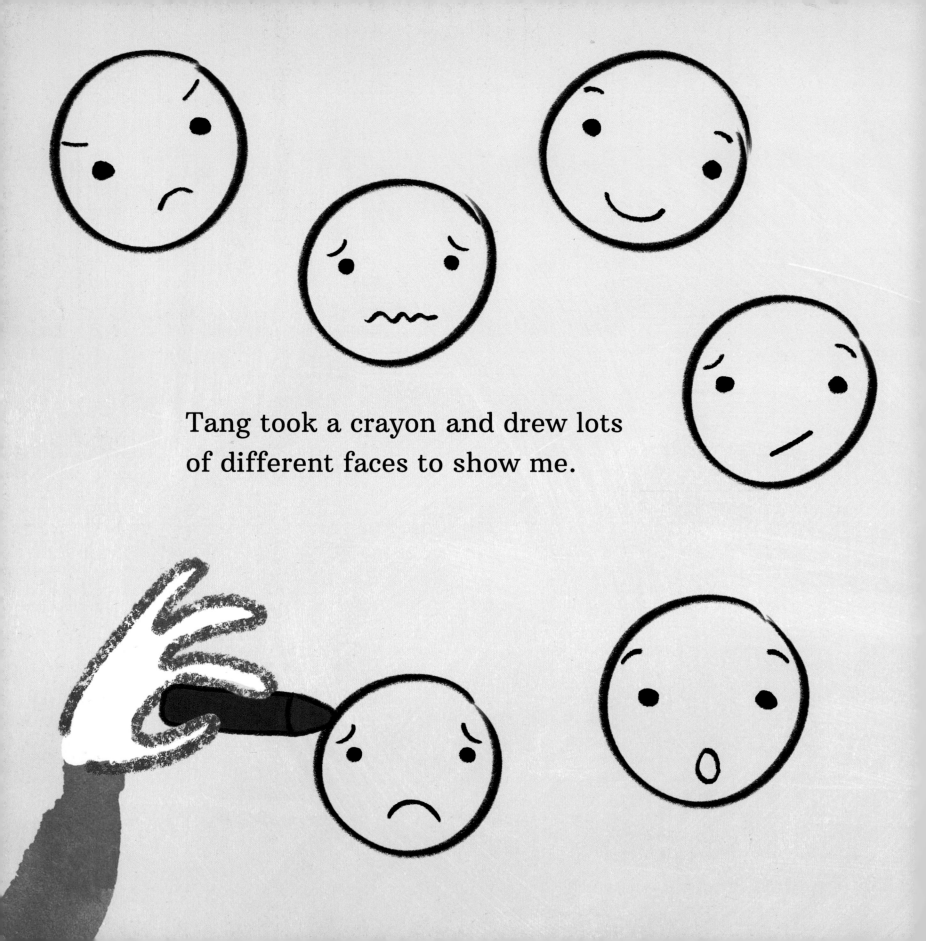

Tang took a crayon and drew lots
of different faces to show me.

"My face is never going to remember to make **all those shapes!**" I sighed.

I was feeling **very** confused. But my face didn't change. "Sometimes my face **forgets** and doesn't do anything, and then I look like this." I said.

"Sorry!" said the Mirror Face. "Sometimes it doesn't seem important to change. And sometimes, when I get tired, I just like to do nothing."

"But, if my face does **nothing,** how will Mum know that I want to play with Lorna?" I asked.

"In point of fact, **words** might come in handy here," said Draff. "Words can name things. And tell you things. And teach you things. **Words** can say all kinds of things, including how you feel, without your face having to do much at all."

Words

Words

Words

Words

Words

"Ooh! Ooh!" said Tang. "That's how Mum will know you want to play with Lorna. You can tell her! With words!"

"Play with Lorna! Play with Lorna!" said Llama excitedly.

But I can't always find my words. I wished there was another way to talk to Mum, without using words . . .

And suddenly, I remembered that there was!

I drew a picture to show Mum
how I was really feeling.

That way, it didn't matter
what my face was doing.
And it didn't matter that I
couldn't find my words!

"Your face is remembering
to smile again!" said Mouse.

My face doesn't always tell people what I am feeling,
and I can't always find my words either . . .

But there are other ways to tell people things . . .
like drawing!

"Oh!" said Mum when she saw my picture. "Is that you and Lorna? Do you want to play with Lorna after all?"

Hooray! I did want to play with Lorna! And this time, Mum knew it!

Soon, Lorna and I were playing.
I showed Lorna my picture, and
we sang my favourite Wren song.

It didn't matter what my face was doing, because Lorna knew I was **happy.**